REAL
FOR SURE
SISTER

REAL
FOR SURE
SISTER

by Ann Angel
Illustrated by Joanne Bowring

Perspectives Press
Fort Wayne, Indiana

Perspectives Press
905 West Wildwood Avenue
Fort Wayne, Indiana 46807

Manufactured in the United States of America
ISBN 0-9609504-7-8

Library of Congress Cataloging-in-Publication Data

Angel, Ann, 1952–
    Real for sure sister.

    Summary: A racially mixed family of adopted
siblings prepares for the arrival of a biracial baby
named Stevi.
    [1. Adoption--Fiction. 2. Brothers and sisters--
Fiction. 3. Family life--Fiction] I. Bowring, Joanne,
ill. II. Title.
PZ7.A5822Re 1988   [Fic]   87-29217
ISBN 0-9609504-7-8

To Jeff, Amanda, Nicky, Joey and Stephanie
Know that I love you.

CHAPTER

"Mom, do you remember when we adopted Joey?" asked Amanda.

"Of course, Honey. Why?" said Amanda's mother as she turned a page of her book. Amanda's mom was sitting in an old wicker rocker on the porch while Amanda lay near her on the porch floor. Crayons and paper were strewn on the floor, under the rocker and across the room. Amanda was supposed to be drawing a picture for her mom— a picture she had been working on all morning. But Amanda was hot and tired and a little bored. She picked up a pink crayon and placed it next to a red one. She picked up a green crayon and rolled it under the rocker. It just missed getting smashed as Amanda's mother rocked back and forth. The crayon rolled to a stop next to a black marker.

"Do you remember how you were gone for a long, long time and I had a stomach ache the whole time you were gone?" Amanda crawled into the rocker with her mother.

Amanda's mom shifted away from her in order to see the book page and said, "I remember."

"Do you think Joey was worth all that bother?" asked Amanda.

Amanda could tell that her mom was getting a little bugged. She pulled a knee up into the rocker, squishing Amanda. Amanda wiggled until her mom put her leg down. "Of course I think Joey was worth it," Amanda's mom said.

"I do too, I just wanted to make sure you did. That's all," said Amanda.

Her mother glanced up from her book and gave Amanda a look that meant, "Go play." When Amanda only wiggled more solidly into the rocker, her mother sighed and put her free arm around her, holding the book up with her other hand. She continued to read.

"That must be a good book you're reading," said Amanda.

"Mmmm," said her mother.

"Is it one I can read when you're finished?" asked Amanda, who loved to read and often read the newspaper over her mom's shoulder.

"Hmmm?" asked Amanda's mom. She didn't really want or expect an answer.

Amanda lazily listened to the outside sounds as she leaned against her mother's side. Stretching one nine-year-old, skinny, tanned leg to the porch floor, she gave a push and set the chair rocking gently. Her thoughts went back to the previous school year and getting Joey.

Amanda remembered how long her parents had been in Mexico to adopt Joey. She had stayed behind with her brother, Nicky, and her Aunt Cindy.

Even though Aunt Cindy was her favorite aunt, it hadn't been any fun to stay at home. Amanda had worried that her parents would get lost or not get the baby. They hadn't even known how to speak Spanish! Every day that passed during the weeks that they were gone had seemed long and scary to Amanda. Her parents had called once and Amanda had asked, "How much longer will you be gone?"

Dad had answered, "As long as it takes, Sweetheart. But trust me. It's worth it. Your new brother is beautiful." And then he had hung up and left Amanda to worry more. At the time she had doubted that any baby could be worth all this trouble. Every morning Amanda would wake up and hope her parents would be home and every morning she would find that she had to wait longer.

Finally, her parents had returned with Amanda's tiny, tired, baby brother. Within days, Amanda knew that her brother had been worth every moment of worry. Joey was as sweet and beautiful as Dad had said. The baby looked at her with his serious black eyes as though he understood everything Amanda said to him and soon he was gurgling and smiling for her.

Now, if Amanda listened carefully, she could hear Joey upstairs in his crib, talking. He was supposed to be asleep. Outside the hot weather bugs, called cicadas, buzzed loud and long. Children's voices could be heard from the sidewalks. Amanda and her mother continued to rock slowly in the chair.

It was the last day of summer vacation. Tomorrow Amanda and Nicky would return to school. Their mother would begin teaching an art course at the community college while Joey stayed with Aunt Cindy.

Amanda was tired of summer games. She could hear Nicky, her seven-year-old brother, as he raced his bike up and down the sidewalk. Ryan, Nicky's best friend, was with him. The two boys were almost always together, thought Amanda. If she stretched her neck and peeked over the porch rail, Amanda could see Nicky's blond hair whizzing by the window. It seemed as if Nicky had spent the whole summer riding past the house. He sure loved to ride his bike. And, thought Amanda, he wasn't looking forward to school tomorrow.

Amanda's summer had been busy, too. She had played with her best friend, Mary Won Hee, whenever she could. They played dolls and school and things like that. Sometimes, Mary Won Hee's two brothers and Nicky would play "Red Rover" and "Statues" with the two girls. Mostly, Amanda had liked helping her mom take care of Joey.

Amanda thought Joey was just about the neatest baby anyone could ever hope to have. Mom and Dad had worked very hard to get him. They had decided to adopt a baby long before Joey finally came into their lives. For months, Amanda's mom had gone to city halls and courts to collect papers for an adoption. She had found a lady who could translate all the English into Spanish. Then she had sent all the papers to an adoption agency. The family had found out about Joey from a social worker who worked at the adoption agency, an agency that helps parents and kids become families.

The story of Joey's birth was very sad. He had been born on a very poor farm in Mexico and his birthmother had died. Joey was so little and hungry that he had almost died too. His birthfather hadn't wanted Joey to die but he had three other sons to care for. Together the father and three boys worked on the farm. There would be no one to stay home and take care of the baby. Finally, Joey's father had walked to the village and asked Madre Carmen, a Catholic nun, to help them find a family for Joseph— a family who could feed him, love him and raise him as their son. Madre Carmen, who often took care of the village's children, brought Joey to a hospital and called the adoption agency. She said this little boy needed a family badly. When the social worker at the agency called Amanda's parents, she said, "Can you go to Mexico and get him?" Mom and Dad had gone to Mexico that week and had stayed until Joey was legally adopted.

"Joey," Amanda's mother often said, "was a true gift of love, just as each of you were."

Amanda sure felt like Joey was a lucky miracle now. He was the happiest baby! Ryan, Nicky's friend, had a baby who cried all the time. Not Joey! You could even ignore him and he was happy. It was just like Dad had said. Joey was worth the wait.

Amanda thought Joey was probably the most beautiful baby in the world, too. He was a Mexican Indian with thick, black hair and the darkest, brightest eyes. Joey's skin was dark brown that turned almost black from the sun.

When he had first come home, Joey had a deep "worry line" on his forehead between his eyebrows. He had been skinny and tiny. Surrounded by his new family, given constant love and attention, he soon became the family's round, happy baby.

The best part was that Joey could say Amanda's name before he was a year old. He would give her hugs and kisses— wet, sloppy kisses— and say "Danda," and he loved Amanda as much as she loved him. Amanda wasn't alone. Everyone who met Joey thought he was a happy baby.

As much as Amanda helped get diapers and make bottles, she couldn't get enough of her little baby, she thought.

"Mom," said Amanda, "do you think we could get another baby, only you wouldn't be gone so long this time?"

Amanda's mother closed her book on her lap and gave Amanda a hug. "Sometimes I'd like another baby, too. But, Amanda, babies are a lot of work and don't just pop up when you want them. We waited five years for you and two for Nicky."

"How long did you wait for Joey?"

"Two years. But, Honey, these days, some parents wait ten years or longer to get babies in the United States. Adopting from another country again would be impossible because it takes a tremendous amount of patience and work and money to get the baby to the United States. Besides, Daddy and I are so busy with you three, we don't have the time or energy to get all the paperwork together again."

"Aren't there any babies in the United States that nobody wants?" asked Amanda.

"I don't think so, Honey."

Amanda leaned against her mother's shoulder. She stretched her toe down to the floor and pushed the rocker to make it rock. Now that she knew how difficult it was to get a baby, she really wished she could have another one. It would be fun. She'd just have to talk it up, work on her mom and dad. After all, Joey was getting so big.

Now that school had started, mornings, and especially breakfast, were busy in Amanda's house. Daddy was always saying he'd be late for work. He gulped his coffee and ate standing up, which bugged Amanda because she knew she'd get yelled at if she ate like that.

Mom, who usually wore her bathrobe, spooned mushy, white cereal into Joey's mouth. In between bites she would put bread in the toaster, then butter it and then put it on plates for Nicky and Amanda, who were usually rushing around looking for their backpacks and books. Now that fall was here, everyone was running into each other looking for sweatshirts and jackets. At the same time, Mom would be calling out, "Nicky, tie your shoes before you fall and kill yourself!" or "Amanda, you can't go to school in purple pants and an orange top!"

Today was even more hectic than usual. Everyone was late getting started. As Amanda's mom was calling upstairs to tell Nicky to hurry up ". . . and don't forget a jacket because it's cold today," the phone rang.

Amanda, who was in the bathroom brushing her teeth, didn't hear the phone conversation. When she came into the kitchen and saw the changes in her mom and dad, she knew she had missed a good phone call, though. She heard her mother say, "... could handle it. I'm sure we could."

Dad was actually sitting down to drink his coffee. He looked thoughtful. "I can't see how we could say 'No,' but it's certainly more than we bargained for."

That seemed to put Mom into an especially happy mood. She leaned over and gave Dad a quick kiss, then danced over to Joey, who was babbling for more cereal.

Nicky came downstairs behind Amanda. He was dressed in a pair of jeans and a t-shirt that somehow looked all crooked on him. His tennis shoes were untied. His yellow hair was sticking up and he didn't look very awake. Nicky didn't seem to like mornings much. He usually ended up needing Mom's help to straighten his clothes out.

"What's up?" asked Amanda as she reached across the table for some orange juice. She hated orange juice, but her mother would stand there to make sure she drank it. "Vitamin C keeps colds away," her mom would say.

"Do you remember how you always ask about more babies?" asked her mom, who didn't give her time to say anything. "Well, I guess sometimes babies come before you know it. So, what would you think if you could have a new brother or sister?"

"That would be nice," said Amanda. "If it was another brother, I'd sure like it."

"This baby would be bi-racial," added Mom.

"What's bi-racial?"

"... a baby who has birthparents who are two different races. This baby has one black birthparent and one white birthparent," said Amanda's dad. Amanda knew a birthparent was the parent who gave a baby life. She had a set of birthparents she had never met. Amanda's parents were her adoptive parents. They hadn't given birth to her, but they had wanted a family to raise and love and had built one by adopting their children. Amanda's best friend, Mary Won Hee, had also been adopted. She was born in a country called Korea. Mary Won Hee's brothers, Doug and Timmy, weren't adopted though. Families, thought Amanda, can sometimes be pretty confusing.

Amanda's dad poured himself another cup of coffee and continued, "The adoption agency that helped us find Joey just called. They need to find a good home for a baby. The baby isn't born yet, but the birthmother knows that she can't take care of it. She asked the agency to help her. She said she was hoping the baby could be a part of a large family and the social worker thought of us."

"I want a new baby," said Amanda. "I think it would be great."

Nicky nodded in agreement. He seemed to like the idea of another baby, but it was hard to tell what Nicky liked, especially in the morning. He looked so tired this morning that Amanda thought he was going to fall back to sleep right in his cereal. Amanda giggled and pushed Nicky's head up. He scowled and continued to eat.

Joey, who was sitting in his yellow high chair, squished warm cereal between his fingers. Unaware that his place in the family was about to change, he chuckled and told his family, "Ucky!"

Amanda, who remembered how long her parents had been gone when they adopted Joey, didn't remember much about her own adoption or Nicky's. "Do you have to go away for a long time to get this baby?" she asked.

Her dad stood to go to work. He kissed Joey, Nicky, and then Amanda on the top of the head. "No, we'd only be gone a few hours. This baby will be born in this state."

"Dad, I think another baby would be a good idea," said Nicky quietly.

Amanda's father turned to her mother and said, "I don't know how we'll handle four children— two of them babies— but call the agency and tell them it looks like we'll do it." And then he was out the door.

Amanda's mom had the biggest, happiest smile on her face. It seemed Amanda wasn't the only one who had been wishing for another baby. She picked Joey up from the high chair, twirled him around and started toward the stairs to get him dressed.

"Don't be pokey, guys. You'll be late for school," she said. As Mom walked past Amanda, she tussled her messy, straight, brown hair with a free hand. "Don't forget to comb that. Nicky, straighten out your shirt before you leave," she added.

Amanda and Nicky sat quietly at the table and finished their breakfast. Nicky took such a long time to wake up, it was better not to talk to him in the morning. Besides, Amanda had a lot to think about today.

She twisted a strand of hair with her finger and wondered what a bi-racial baby would look like— maybe a checkerboard or stripes, or maybe like a black person only with light skin, or like a white person with dark brown skin.

Amanda had some brown friends at school. They all had brown parents. Sometimes kids would tease them about the color of their skin— just because it was different than their own. Amanda would always stick up for her friends. She wondered if she would get hurt feelings if people teased her about a brown brother or sister. She thought she would. Amanda figured that someday she would find out, because, as her mother always said, kids love to tease.

Joey was a brown Indian. Amanda wasn't sure what color his birthparents had been, but she thought her mom had told her they were Indians too. Amanda thought she'd ask to make sure.

"Are you excited about the baby?" Amanda asked Nicky.

Nicky really hated to think in the morning. He rubbed his eyes and mumbled, "I guess so."

"Gee, you're no fun in the morning, Nicky," said Amanda. She decided not to ask Nicky any more questions. She decided to figure it out for herself. Besides, she was older and she should know more than Nicky anyway.

People are all different but the same, she thought. Some of the people in her family had blue eyes and Amanda had brown eyes. Joey's eyes were almost black. Everyone in Amanda's family had dark hair, except Nicky. He had blond hair. Most of us have teeth, she thought. But Nicky knocked his teeth out when he got hit with a teeter totter and Joey cried sometimes because his teeth were growing. Her dad had a gold tooth. Amanda thought that when she got married, she'd marry a man with a gold tooth. It looked really cool. Sooner or later, thought Amanda, we all have teeth and hair and look pretty much the same when it comes to important stuff like arms and legs and ears. Amanda decided the new baby would look the same but different, too. It would probably have curly brown hair and light brown skin. She thought she'd probably get mad if anyone ever teased her about Joey or Nicky or the new baby. So far, nobody had said anything mean about Joey. Amanda's friend, Sally, had once called Nicky a brat. But he was being a brat.

"Nicky, you're going to be late for school," said Amanda. "Can you tell Mom that I left already?"

As Nicky nodded his head in reply, Amanda grabbed her jacket and backpack and opened the front door. She stepped off the porch into bright sunlight. Amanda could tell it was going to be a beautiful day. The trees were covered with red and gold leaves. Even though there was a chill in the air, it was warm for October.

Yes, this was going to be a good day— a good baby kind of day, thought Amanda. If she hurried, she could walk with Sally to school. She'd have time to talk to both Sally and Mary Won Hee before the bell rang. She could tell them all about her new baby.

CHAPTER

The week before Amanda's new baby came, a social worker paid a visit. It was an Indian Summer day. Amanda's dad came home to see the social worker. They were going to have a picnic on the patio.

"Dad," said Amanda as she held the screen door open for her father, "What's a social worker?"

Amanda's dad walked outside carrying a dish of pickles and a straw basket of potato chips. He set them on the white umbrella table and began to stick paper napkins under plates. "A social worker is a person who went to college and learned all about families and society," he said. "Our social worker, the same one who came here to meet you before we got Joey, is an adoption social worker. Her job is to make families who wish to adopt ready for their children. She also helps birthmothers and their families make a plan— like adoption— for their children."

Amanda's dad always gave long answers. She thought she would ask her mom tough questions from now on because Amanda was never quite sure what her dad's long answers meant.

Amanda wondered, if the social worker helped make adoption plans for babies, did this mean the social worker also decided which parents and families were good enough to get babies?

Amanda was going to ask her mom, but Mom was busy getting Joey and Nicky cleaned up at the kitchen sink. She wasn't going to ask her dad. She probably wouldn't understand his answer.

Amanda figured she should be on her best behavior. She told Nicky, "You better be extra nice or we won't get the baby. Then you'll be the middle child forever." Amanda didn't know what the big deal about a middle child was, but she had heard her mom and dad talking about middle children with their friends. It seemed like it was the wrong place to be.

Amanda and Nicky helped their parents make a picnic in the backyard. Mom made sure Joey was in his best play clothes. Then she sent Amanda and Nicky upstairs to change into clean play clothes. Amanda put on her rainbow sun dress that had red ribbons that tied on her shoulders.

"Don't forget," said Amanda to Nicky on their way downstairs, "be extra good."

When the social worker knocked on the front door, Amanda ran to answer it. She was very polite even though she had to push Nicky away so she could answer the door. "Hi. Do you remember me? I don't think I remember you," she said. "My name's Amanda. My brother's name is Nicky. My other brother is Joey," she continued until her mother interrupted with "Come on in, Liz."

The social worker seemed nice to Amanda. Liz was about Mom's age. She told Nicky and Amanda to call her by her first name. She was tall and thin and smiled a lot. Amanda thought Liz liked kids. She talked directly to Amanda and Nicky— a lot of people don't. For instance, she had noticed that old Mrs. Delaney who lived across the street only pretended to be polite to kids but she never really looked at them unless it was to see how dirty they were. Liz asked Amanda all kinds of questions about school and her friends. She asked Amanda what was the best part of having her brothers and then she asked Amanda if she wanted the new baby to be a boy or girl. Liz explained that the baby hadn't been born yet, but was due to be born any day now. Amanda told Liz she wanted a boy.

Everybody else said they didn't care if the baby was a boy or girl as long as it was healthy. Amanda thought, I bet that's what you're supposed to say.

She really wanted a boy though. She didn't want someone to wear her baby dresses that were all put away in plastic bags in the attic. She didn't want someone to borrow her dolls and stuff. A boy would be great. Nicky and Joey could just keep sharing all their junk. Besides Grandma and Grandpa liked to buy pretty dresses and hair ribbons for Amanda. They bought metal trucks and other boring things for the boys.

Grandma always said, "You're the first little girl I've ever had to shop for." Grandma didn't have any daughters.

If Amanda had a baby sister, Grandma and Grandpa might only buy half the pretty things for her and half for the new baby. No, Amanda didn't want a sister.

Liz's lunch visit was over all too soon. Amanda and Nicky walked her to her car and waved good-bye. As Liz's car turned the corner, Nicky said, "Boy, did you mess up! You shoulda' told Liz you'd take a boy or girl. She's going to think you're awful picky. Besides, she saw you push me to let her in."

Amanda started to worry that even though she had been polite, she had said the wrong thing when she said she only wanted a boy. Maybe Nicky was right. She had messed up. She worried that Liz would think they weren't a perfect family so there wouldn't be any more babies— even if the baby was a boy. Amanda worried that her family would be angry because of what she said.

At dinner, Amanda wasn't hungry. She pushed her potatoes and peas around her plate and said, "No thank you" when her mother asked her if she wanted some ice cream for dessert.

Amanda worried that Liz might call and say, "I'm sorry, but your daughter Amanda is so picky we're not going to let you have any more babies. Besides, she pushes her brother, Nicky, around."

At bedtime, Amanda couldn't get to sleep. She remembered that Mom had once said that after an adoption is final in court, you're a real family for ever and ever. No matter what. Amanda worried that her mother had been wrong and that wasn't so. Maybe, thought Amanda, I was so horrible the social worker will come and take Joey and Nicky away from me. Worse, maybe the social worker would come and take Amanda!

She scurried out of bed and ran into her mom and dad's bedroom. Amanda was crying now. She was frightened and miserable.

Amanda's mom woke up and put her arms around Amanda. She pulled her into the big, warm bed. "What is it, Honey? Why are you so frightened?"

"I did something horrible!" said Amanda. "I'm so mean! I told Liz I only wanted a baby boy and now she'll probably come and put me in a home where I won't be so selfish! She might take the boys!"

"Oh, Honey," said Mom, "no one will ever take the boys and they won't ever take you. Sometimes, at night, you do let your imagination run away. We'll always be a family."

Amanda was still worried and upset. She said, "But Liz won't think we're perfect anymore because of what I said and, besides, I pushed Nicky. We won't get any more babies, I just know it!"

Amanda's mom said, "Don't worry, Honey." She always called Amanda "Honey." "They don't just give babies to perfect families or perfect parents. If that were the case, we wouldn't have three kids. You only have to try to be the best you can be . . . and you were only being honest."

Amanda thought about that. She thought her mom might be right. After all, Mom wasn't perfect. Her mom sure could yell when she was mad.

"Do you think that Liz would let us have a baby if she knew that you yell, and, once, when Nicky put dish soap in the clothes washer, you said a swear word?"

"Yes, Amanda," said her mom. "Liz understands that parents can get frustrated."

"Do you think that Liz would let us have a baby if she knew that Joey bit me so hard we couldn't make him let me go?"

"Yes, Amanda. Liz understands that."

"Do you think," asked Amanda with a grin on her face and a glint in her brown eyes, "she'd let us have a baby if you bit me?"

"Go to bed Amanda," said her mother as she pulled the covers from Amanda and gave her a gentle push out of bed. "I love you, silly," she added.

Amanda went back to her bed. She felt better after their talk. Amanda curled into her cozy, warm bed and thought, "Dear God, I'll never just want a brother again . . . a sister is fine, too."

It seems God heard her prayer. That very night, Amanda's baby sister was born.

"I have a baby sister, and she's coming home today. I have a new sister," chanted Amanda as she pranced and danced around her bedroom.

She went to the mirror and inspected herself. No, her blue sweater was all wrong. Amanda would dress to celebrate today. She peeled off her sweater and threw it to the floor. The sweater settled on a pile of baby clothes she had been inspecting the night before. She reached into the open dresser drawer and pulled out her pink sweater— the one with snow stars across the front.

Amanda's mom and dad were driving to another city to pick the baby up today. Amanda had decided she was perfectly happy with a new sister, especially since she had learned the baby would be sleeping in Joey's room.

The new baby's name was Stephanie Jean— Stevi for short.

The doorbell rang. Amanda ran a comb through her hair and raced to see if Aunt Kim had arrived to babysit while Mom and Dad were gone.

It was Kim, one of Mom's many sisters. She was standing in the doorway. The whole family was already downstairs and everyone was talking at once— even Joey, who was sitting on the bottom step.

Amanda's parents were all dressed up and both talking in an attempt to give Aunt Kim instructions. Nicky, big as he was getting, was hanging on Kim's arm.

"Nicky," said Amanda as she hopped off the last step. "Mom and Dad told you not to hang on people. You're too big."

Amanda waited for her parents to stop talking. She wanted to ask them when they'd be home. They kept talking and talking. Even when Amanda finally interrupted everyone kept talking. Amanda wanted to know if she and Nicky could come home for lunch, but it was too noisy to ask. She wondered if maybe she could stay home from school and wait for the baby, but no one would listen.

"Is it cold out, Kim?" asked Amanda's mom when she noticed the heavy coat Kim was wearing. "I'll get a heavier blanket for the baby."

She turned and walked up the stairs. Kim followed.

"Kim, Kim," called Nicky, who should have been getting ready for school. "Can we color?"

"Come here, Joey," said Amanda's dad as he swung Joey into his arms. "Let's get your Cheerios. Amanda, let's get moving. You have school," he called over his shoulder.

Amanda followed her dad and stood at the kitchen table where he placed a bowl of cereal and a spoon. She stood as she ate, just like her dad usually did, and wolfed down her cereal. She grabbed her backpack from the counter and stomped out of the kitchen.

Amanda was a little angry that no one was paying any attention to her. "Good-by. Good-by. Have a nice day, Amanda," called Amanda as she grabbed her red winter jacket from the hook near the back door and shoved her arms into it. "Hmphh, last year's coat and it's too small," said Amanda in an irritated and loud voice. "I bet all the kids at school will notice." She slammed the back door as she left the house.

Amanda had started to feel a lot like she didn't want a new baby girl. Everybody was so busy getting ready for Stevi, she felt they had forgotten all about her and Nicky and Joey.

Amanda knew her mom and dad had to go to another city to pick Stevi up from a foster home. Her mom had told her foster homes were places where people take care of children until the parents can bring them home. Amanda had wanted to know just how long her parents would be gone. She was not happy that she was being ignored. Not at all happy!

Mom was so busy getting the new baby stuff into the car parked near the sidewalk that she almost didn't see Amanda as she walked past. But she did and said, "Have a good day. We'll be home in time for supper tonight. I love you . . ." and into the car she went, and off she and Dad went, and . . . and Amanda felt like she was going to cry. She felt all alone. It wasn't as bad, though, as when Mom and Dad had gone to Mexico to adopt Joey.

After all, Amanda knew her parents would be back at dinnertime. Her mom had said so.

School seemed awfully long today. Amanda didn't feel like doing her work. She kept wondering what her new baby would look like. Mrs. Murphy's voice buzzed and droned in the background, but Amanda didn't listen. She wrote a note to her friend, Sally, during math and told her about the baby. During reading, she whispered to Mary Won Hee that the baby was coming home. At recess, she told Richard and Gwen and Terry that she was getting a new baby and her name was going to be Stephanie. As the day wore on, Amanda forgot all about being ignored that morning and became more and more excited. She told all her friends that she was getting a new baby sister. Many of the kids didn't believe Amanda though. Only Mary Won Hee understood how Amanda's mom could have a baby without getting a fat tummy.

Amanda and Mary Won Hee were very busy explaining all about adoption, when Mrs. Murphy, who was trying to teach geography, interrupted.

"Amanda," she said in a not-very-pleasant voice. "What is so important that you have to talk right now?" Mrs. Murphy's brown eyes glared over her glasses. "Why don't you share your important secret with the class?"

Amanda knew Mrs. Murphy didn't really expect her to share a secret with the class, but it was her chance to explain about her baby sister. Amanda stood up, faced the class, and announced, "I'm getting a new, brown baby sister today. She's coming from a city up north. We're adopting her. This means she has two sets of parents, my mom said— like everyone in my family. The new baby has

a set of parents who gave her life and my parents, who are
going to be her mom and dad."

Amanda gulped air and looked toward Mrs. Murphy.
She was smiling now and nodded her head in encourage-
ment. "Tell us more, dear," said Mrs. Murphy.

Amanda told her class how her parents were her real parents— just adopted— and her brothers and sister were her real brothers and sister— just adopted. She didn't tell them that if anybody ever says, "Your brothers and sister aren't your real for sure brothers and sister," she'd punch them in the nose, but, she thought, she would punch them right in the nose.

The school day passed.

Amanda raced home as fast as she could. Kim was still there. Although Kim was her favorite aunt— all Amanda's aunts were her favorite aunts— she was disappointed. Amanda had hoped the new baby would be home.

Amanda ate brownies and told Aunt Kim about how the kids at school hadn't believed about the new baby.

"I have to get my markers now," she said. "I'm going to make a welcome home sign." Amanda wrote "Welcome Baby Stevi" in big, round letters. Nicky and Aunt Kim helped her color it in.

Then they waited. They waited a long time. Amanda was sure her mother had said she'd be home for dinner, but dinner came and went. Aunt Kim made hamburgers. The only one who was hungry was Joey. He ate all his dinner and most of Amanda's. Amanda always gave Joey food she didn't like.

Amanda and Nicky helped Aunt Kim with the dishes. They watched the sky grow dark. They were getting tired of waiting. Finally, the back door opened and Daddy walked in. It was so good to see him. Amanda noticed he had a big smile on his face. "Say hello to Stephanie Jean," he said. Mom walked in the door. She was holding a lumpy, pink blanket that moved.

Amanda ran to the blanket and peeked into it. She thought her new baby was really, really pretty. Her bright brown eyes were looking right at Amanda. She had fat cheeks.

The baby's hair stuck out all over like she had been caught in the wind, or something. The baby's hair wasn't curly at all, but, thought Amanda, she sure was pretty.

Nicky and Amanda both got to hold Stevi, who looked like a Stevi should look. When Mom tried to help Joey look at the baby, he acted jealous and pushed her away.

Nothing bothered Stevi though. She fell asleep in Nicky's arms and didn't wake up again. Amanda touched Stevi's cheeks with her fingers and the baby slept soundly. Mom sat, curled on the floor, holding the sleeping baby. A very tired Joey leaned against her, drinking his bottle. It was time for bed.

While Amanda said her prayers, she told God she thought she was going to like Stevi a lot. "Oh, and thank you, God," she said as she drifted off to sleep.

Christmas is everywhere, thought Amanda as she walked through the shopping mall. Gold stars, as big as Joey, hung from the ceiling. "Silent Night" played over the intercom. Here and there were mechanical elves and fairies in snow covered houses.

Joey, tucked in the twin stroller, pointed and "Oohed." His brown eyes were wide, happy buttons. "Joey," said Amanda, "Look at the candy cane entrance. Santa's in there!"

Baby Stevi snuggled in a blanket, sucking a pacifier, and stared at all the bright things. She and Joey faced each other in the stroller.

"Nicky," said Amanda's mom as she pushed the stroller. "Don't touch everything."

Nicky, as usual, was walking in a zig zag so he could see and touch the decorations. As his mother pushed the stroller, she would reach out and pull Nicky to her side. "Can I see Santa? Do you think I can have these race cars? Isn't that neat?" asked Nicky of no one in particular.

The excitement of the season had certainly taken hold.

"Mom, I don't think Dad liked the pink tie I got him last year," said Amanda. "Do you think I could get him some records? I already know what I'm getting you," she added.

Amanda's mom made a face that meant she was getting tired of all the chatter. "I think you can get Daddy some tapes for Christmas, but will you let me help pick them out, Honey? . . . Nicky! Please don't put your hands through the elves' windows. If the store owners saw you, they'd make us leave!"

Nicky, curious as ever, was trying to see if there was glass in the windows of the elves' cottages. There wasn't.

"Who wants a Coke?" asked Amanda's mom.

Mom and Nicky went over to a bright orange pizza stand. They returned shortly with three paper cups that had straws sticking out of the top. "Let's sit at that bench," said Mom pointing a paper cup toward a rest area.

As Amanda sat, sipping her drink, she watched the people go by. It seemed as though everyone had an armful of presents and bags. Although it was warm inside the mall, people were bundled in coats and hats. A grandpa came past with a large bag from the sporting goods store. Amanda thought he had probably bought his grandchildren ice skates or a football. What a nice man, she thought.

"Oh, oh," said Amanda. "Look who's here and I think she sees us." Old Mrs. Delaney, their neighbor, walked out of the shoe store and straight toward Amanda and her family.

"Oh, no," muttered Nicky, who didn't like Mrs. Delaney any better than Amanda did. They both thought she was a busybody, but Mom was always telling them to be nice to Mrs. Delaney. "She's a poor, lonely woman who means well," Amanda's mom would say.

Amanda looked over at her mother in time to see a frown cross her face. It was replaced quickly with a smile.

"Well, well," said Mrs. Delaney, who smelled like an old closet. "I see you're doing your Christmas shopping. I'm so pleased to run into you. I haven't seen your new little one, although I've certainly heard a lot about her."

I bet, thought Amanda. You probably heard about our baby and wondered how Mom could ever keep all of us clean and well behaved.

Amanda was sure that Mrs. Delaney was not a poor, lonely old lady. She was sure that Mrs. Delaney was a lady who was concerned only with keeping the whole world in order. Amanda was positive that Mrs. Delaney thought the world would be a cleaner, much neater place if there were no children in it.

Amanda's mom leaned over the stroller and pulled the pink blanket from Stevi's sleeping face. Joey had pulled the pacifier from Stevi's mouth and was sucking it as he nodded off to sleep.

"This is our littlest," said Amanda's mother proudly. "Her name is Stephanie Jean but the kids call her Stevi."

"These children are so lucky," said Mrs. Delaney, who barely glanced at the baby. "The poor things would probably have terrible lives if you hadn't come along."

"No," said Amanda's mom with a smile. "They would have gone to the next people on a very long list of people waiting for children."

Amanda felt uncomfortable. She wished people like Mrs. Delaney wouldn't talk about adoption like it was a special favor to kids. My parents are lucky, too. Not many people are lucky enough to have such wonderful children, she thought. Mom tells us that. I wish she'd tell Mrs. Delaney.

"She's a very pretty baby," said Mrs. Delaney as she finally inspected the brown skinned, fuzzy-haired baby. "I suppose people are always asking where you got these two," she added. "I was just telling the girl who does my hair about you nice people and how you adopted a Mexican baby and then a black baby. She knows a couple who have been waiting to adopt for years."

Amanda glanced at Nicky. Like Amanda, he hated being treated differently just because he was adopted. Nicky was staring at Mrs. Delaney with an icy blue-eyed stare. Amanda realized her mother didn't look too happy either.

"It was good to see you," said Amanda's mom as she stood and began to button her coat. "We have a lot to do today."

Mrs. Delaney ignored the gentle hint. She brushed imagined lint from the hem of her black coat. "My girl at the beauty shop said this couple had tried for years to have children of their own. She asked if that was your case. You know, I really couldn't answer her, dear. Could you have children of your own?"

"I have four children of my own," said Amanda's mother with a wide smile. "Come on kids. We have lots to do for Christmas," she said without so much as a good-by to Mrs. Delaney.

Amanda and Nicky grinned triumphantly as they followed their mom out of the mall.

In the car on the way home, Amanda said, "That mean old Mrs. Delaney sure look surprised when you walked away from her. I can't stand her. She makes it sound like we don't really belong to anybody."

"Amanda, I know it's hard for you to hear people talk like that. You too, Nicky. I don't like it either, but kids,

they just don't know any better."

"I don't think Mrs. Delaney has had many people in her life to love her. I don't think she knows a whole lot about family love," she added.

"I don't think I can like Mrs. Delaney though, Mom," said Nicky.

"I don't want to understand her," added Amanda. She listened to the quiet inside the car. Joey was humming softly in the back seat as the tires splashed slushy water against the car.

Right now, thought Amanda, I love Joey and Stevi and Nicky more than ever. I won't ever let anyone make them feel like they don't belong.

"I especially hate the way Mrs. Delaney talks about Joey and Stevi just because they're different colors. When they get bigger, stuff like she says is going to make them feel bad," said Amanda.

"Oh, Honey," said Amanda's mom, "I hate it, too. I think the important thing is that we're surrounded by family love. Maybe if we let people know how hurtful the things they say are, they'll get the message."

Amanda didn't think Mrs. Delaney would ever get the message. We're not so different from other families that people need to make such a big deal about it, she thought. After all, we love each other a lot— just like every other family.

"Sometimes," said Amanda, "I pretend you're my birthmother and I don't want people to know I'm adopted because they treat me different. Is that O.K?

"Of course it is, Honey," said Amanda's mother. "I would have been very proud to carry all four of you under my heart."

Amanda felt warm and safe and good. I guess it doesn't really matter what people like old Mrs. Delaney say, thought Amanda. The important thing is that we love each other so much and take good care of each other.

6
CHAPTER

"Do I have chocolate on my face, Mary Won Hee?" asked Amanda as she licked a fudge-covered spoon.

"No. Why did you ask me that, Amanda?" asked Mary Won Hee, Amanda's best friend ever.

"You do," said Amanda and burst into a fit of giggles. She giggled more as Mary jumped off the kitchen stool and plotched more chocolate on her nose with a waving spatula. Mary saw her reflection in the oven door. Now both girls held their stomachs as they laughed and giggled. Chocolate dripping from the countertops to the floor set them into new fits of laughter. The kitchen and the girls were a mess. Silly with excitement because Mary was sleeping over, the girls continued to hoot and howl.

Amanda's mom, hearing the giggling girls, came into the room.

"Oh, oh," said a suddenly serious-faced Amanda.

"Oh boy," said Mom as she took in the terrible kitchen disaster. "What a mess. I'll tell you what, if you two go somewhere and play, I'll clean this up."

Knowing good luck when they found it, the girls washed their faces, checked the fudge hardening in the refrigerator and ran upstairs to Amanda's room. Amanda punched the play button on her tape player and the room filled with the sounds of rock and roll. Amanda and Mary dropped onto Amanda's bed and burst into giggles again.

"Danda," called Joey as he toddled unsteadily into the room. "Dance, Dance."

Joey loved Amanda so much he followed her everywhere, especially if he heard her music. Most of the time, Amanda loved the attention. Today she wanted to be alone with her best friend, Mary Won Hee.

Suddenly, Nicky zipped into the room and wiggled and pranced to the music.

"OUT! OUT!" yelled Amanda as she stood like a soldier, arm out, her finger pointed at the open door. "BUG OFF!" she added loudly and then pushed Nicky out of the room.

As if pulled by a rubber band, Nicky turned and bounced back.

"Mom," called Amanda. "MOM!"

"Watch this, Mary Won Hee," said Nicky as he wiggled and wobbled to the music.

Amanda rolled her eyes. Mary Won Hee did the same.

"Nicky," said Amanda. "You are so weird. Get out of my room . . . and take Joey with you!"

Nicky stopped in the middle of his dance. "I want to stay."

"You are a pain. OUT!" repeated Amanda.

Amanda's mom appeared. She looked tired as she held Stevi on her hip. Amanda had noticed that, lately, Stevi was only happy if she was being held or chewing on her pacifier. Mom said it was because she was teething.

"Baby, Babe," cooed Joey as he waddled to his mother and the baby.

"Come on Nicky. Leave the girls alone," said Mom. She took Joey's hand. "Come on boys. You're not appreciated here."

The two girls turned to the more important task of combing their hair and "getting beautiful" as Amanda's dad liked to say.

"Sometimes," said Amanda, "I wish I was an only child."

"For sure," said her friend. Thoughtfully Mary added, "Nicky sure looked sad when you made him leave."

"I know, but he always acts so dumb around my friends. I get really mad at him."

"I get just the opposite," said Mary. She posed in front of the mirror. Mary Won Hee was a tiny, black-haired, black-eyed nine year old. "Doug and Timmy call me 'Twerp,' and tell me to 'Get lost' all the time . . . just because I'm the baby of the family. I hate it when they do that."

"Once," said Amanda, "I was going to tell Nicky that I hated him because he made me fall off my bike. I didn't because it would have made him feel really bad. But I did kind of hate him for a minute."

Amanda didn't tell Mary Won Hee that she had also kept quiet because she had been afraid her mother would get mad if Nicky told. Instead Amanda had pushed Nicky down. Nicky had told Mom and Amanda had gotten into trouble anyway.

Amanda brushed her hair into a pony tail and tied a blue ribbon in it. "Do you think kids who grow up in their birth families ever feel like they hate each other?" she asked.

"Doug and Timmy do. And my mom said she fought with her brother the whole time they were growing up. They were a birth family. What do you think?"

"I think everybody fights once in a while. But brothers are the worst. They pick on girls." Even as Amanda said these words she realized that Nicky hadn't been picking on her. He had just wanted to be included. Talking about brothers and fighting made Amanda feel bad for Nicky. Maybe, she thought, she should give him a chance.

"Let's go downstairs, get Nicky and ask my mom if we can eat the fudge we made," she said.

The girls included Nicky. The three ate lots and lots of gooey fudge and played what seemed like a hundred games of Chinese Checkers.

Finally, it was bedtime. A hall light shone into the darkened room. The girls were settled under a pink, flowered quilt in Amanda's double bed.

"Mary, are you asleep?" asked Amanda.

"No."

"Do you ever wonder what it would be like to know your birth family in Korea?"

"Yeah. My mom said my birthmother was poor and couldn't take care of me the way she wanted. But sometimes I pretend my birthparents are a king and queen and they gave me away to save me from an attacking army."

"I pretend my birthmother is a famous rock singer," said Amanda. "When I grow up, we meet and sing together on a big stage. I'm pretty sure I'm going to be a singer when I grow up."

"I pretend that my birthparents find me after I'm in college," said Mary. "I'm studying to be a doctor. They just want to know I'm O.K. They don't want to take me away or anything. They're real proud of me." Mary Won Hee propped herself up on her elbow. "They go back to their kingdom and they're happy and I'm happy because I know they're safe and I stay with my real family."

Mary sat up and wrapped her arms around her bended knees. "Do you ever wish you lived with your birthmother?"

"When I'm mad at my family," said Amanda as she copied Mary's position. "But then I'd miss my family."

"Did you know," added Amanda in a softer voice, "Stevi's not ours for sure yet. She's only a foster baby for a waiting period. In May, we can legally adopt her."

"Could her birthmother take her back now?" asked Mary very seriously.

"My mom said that wouldn't happen because Stevi's birthmother already made her decision and told a judge in court that she wanted Stevi to have a mom and dad. I asked my mom if that meant it could never happen. She said it wouldn't. But she didn't say it absolutely wouldn't."

"Do you worry about it?"

"You bet. Stevi cries a lot because she's teething and a baby, but I love her. When I think about it, I think it would be horrible if she didn't become my real for sure sister forever. Sometimes, I even ignore her and pretend she isn't here so I know how bad it would be."

"Don't worry, Amanda," said Mary Won Hee as she patted Amanda's back. "It won't happen. Besides, you told me her birthmother is too young."

Just a few more months, thought Amanda, then she'll be ours.

Amanda thought over all the things she and Mary Won Hee could talk about. She was very lucky to have a friend who understood her so well. She realized they both knew that being adopted doesn't make you different from other kids, it's just a little more complicated.

Amanda knew that she was loved very much and so was Mary Won Hee and that's what's most important. Amanda felt good when she thought about this.

"Let's sneak downstairs and eat the rest of the fudge," she said as she stood and threw the blanket off Mary Won Hee.

The two girls tiptoed into the kitchen and, amidst giggles and whispered "Shss's," they finished off the fudge.

"Please, Honey. Watch the baby while I finish painting Nicky's room," pleaded Amanda's paint spattered mother in a tone that meant Amanda had no choice.

"Mo-o-om. I want to go out and play. Besides she cries too much."

"Amanda, please. I didn't expect her to wake up so soon. I only need about an hour."

"She's not even my real sister yet," said a pouting Amanda. Amanda was referring to the fact that Baby Stevi wouldn't be legally adopted until May— almost two months away. Amanda had recently decided that she would ignore the baby just in case things didn't work out. That way, she reasoned, she wouldn't love the baby too much. Besides Stevi had turned into a real crank since she had begun teething.

"AMANDA," said her mother, looking more than a little angry. "She certainly is your sister. So get used to it. I suggest you go watch her and get to know her better!"

Amanda realized her mother was in no mood to argue. She grudgingly gave in. "O.K. Fine," she said. "But remember, I'm tired of babies. I don't ever want another one." Amanda turned on her heel and went to release the crying baby from her crib.

Amanda was not feeling very happy or, for that matter, loved today. Her two brothers had gone off with Dad to run errands at the office. Mom had immediately put the baby to bed and begun painting. No one had paid any attention to her. Until now. Now her mother would notice her because she needed help with the very fussy baby, Stuff-ini.

"Come on, Steph-the-Wreck," said Amanda as she looked at the disheveled and whimpering baby in her arms. "I'll fix you up a little."

"You're a mess," said Amanda as she took the baby downstairs and plopped her in front of the television. Amanda turned the TV on and flipped the switch to MTV. "Mom won't care. She's busy painting," she said to no one in particular as she opened drawers and collected combs, ribbons and barrettes from the kitchen and bathroom cupboards.

Amanda returned to MTV and Baby Stevi. She inspected her charge. Stevi's nose was running. She was sucking on her fingers and drool dripped onto her bib. Stevi's hair— now there was a lifelong problem— was fuzzy as cotton candy and sticking straight up. Amanda's mother said Stevi's hair looked so funny because she probably had her black birthfather's hair texture without his curls. Amanda thought Stevi would probably spend her life savings on lotions and things to make her hair curly and cute.

"I'll make you as cute as I can," said Amanda, and she left the room for more supplies.

Baby Stevi, unaware that she was about to be the subject of Amanda's beauty experiments, cooed and gurgled at the lady rock star who was strutting across the screen.

Amanda returned shortly with an assortment of things. She set right to work. Off with the bib and shirt. On with the pink dress and tights despite Stevi's whining protests.

"Oooh, you look so pretty," cooed Amanda as she combed and curled Stevi's gel-covered hair. Stevi merely stared at MTV.

When Stevi's curls were in perfect order, Amanda searched through her special box until she found her wide pink ribbon. She wrapped the ribbon around the baby's head and tied it into a big, floppy bow at the top.

Stevi, enthralled with a costumed rock band on TV, didn't seem to notice the bow hanging down to one eyebrow.

Amanda reached into her special box and pulled out a pair of white sunglasses with heart shaped lenses. She placed them squarely on the baby's nose. "Oh, you're so gorgeous. Simply gorgeous. A princess if I ever saw one," exclaimed Amanda.

Baby Stevi seemed to agree as she grinned her two-toothed grin. She didn't even try to take the glasses off her face.

"MOM," called Amanda. "MOM. Come here." Amanda wanted her mother to see the beautiful baby princess.

"What is it, Honey?" called Amanda's mom from upstairs.

"I want you to see the baby."

"Can't it wait? I'm almost finished."

Amanda didn't answer. Fine, she thought. I'll find someone who appreciates us. Amanda decided to take the baby for a walk.

As she opened the back door, Amanda noticed her mother's red sunglasses. She put them on, then rummaged through her mom's purse for lipstick. She added red-orange lipstick to her lips and cheeks. Amanda found a wide-brimmed straw hat and added it to her outfit. Beautiful, she thought.

After adjusting the baby in the stroller, Amanda returned to the house and grabbed her mother's large, full purse. She pulled the strap over her shoulder and the two set off for a little adventure.

It was a warm, March day, a perfect sunny day for a walk. The trees were outlined with green buds and birds were chirping. All the neighbors were outside. As Amanda pushed the baby down the sidewalk, she noticed old Mrs. Delaney, whom she thought she would never like, raking her garden. Amanda turned in the opposite direction. She turned the corner. Sally's house was all closed up. The family had gone out of town for the weekend. Mrs. Krueger was cleaning last year's leaves out of her flower beds. Mr. Clark was helping his son, Kevin, learn to ride a two wheeler.

Baby Stevi gurgled and grinned and held on to the sides of the stroller. She sure liked her walk. Amanda walked and walked, away from her block, across the street and over a few blocks, up a side street and back to her own street. She had walked for quite a while.

Mrs. McCarthy, who was the nicest neighbor ever and always gave Amanda and Nicky cookies, was outside talking to Mrs. Delaney. Amanda looked around. There was no way to get back to the house without talking to Mrs. Delaney. Well, she thought, at least Mrs. McCarthy's there. She decided she would have to talk to them.

"Well, hello dear," said Mrs. McCarthy as she observed the costumes on the two girls. "And who is this lovely creature?" she asked, pointing to the baby.

Amanda said, in her most important and smart voice, "Her name is Princess Stuff-ini because she's a sniveling brat, a very spoiled child. When she grows up it will be difficult for her because she's so spoiled. She wants everything she sees and whines so very much."

Even the usually crabby Mrs. Delaney smiled at this silliness. "Oh what a dear!" she exclaimed to Mrs. McCarthy.

Amanda continued, "We would probably have to pay a prince to marry her, but we won't be able to afford it. Designer jeans are so expensive these . . ."

Amanda stopped in mid-sentence as she heard her mother calling her.

"Amanda Louise!"

Was she ever going to get it now! Amanda had left the yard without telling her mother where she was going. She'd been gone a long time.

"I have to go now," she said as she turned the stroller toward her house. Mom was standing at the front door, her hands on her hips.

"Oh boy," muttered Amanda as she turned up the walk. She had been gone so long she had probably worried her mother. She knew she should have told her mother she was going for a walk. Amanda thought she would get yelled at, maybe sent to her room. She tried to look as sorry as possible and she thought up an explanation for leaving without telling her mother.

"I'm sorry, Mom," she said. "I was just trying to get to know Stevi better, like you told me . . ."

Amanda stopped, surprised.

Her mother wasn't angry! She had heard Amanda talking to the neighbors, but it hadn't prepared her for the way the two girls looked. When Amanda's mother observed the sunglasses, the oversized hat and the floppy, pink ribbon hanging in the baby's eyes, she burst out laughing.

8

CHAPTER

It was May, and, finally, Stevi was going to be legally adopted. Amanda sighed with relief as she walked with her family down the long courthouse hallway. She had thought this day would never come. For weeks, she had worried that something would happen. Maybe Stevi's birthmother would change her mind, or Amanda's parents would decide that four children were too many. Amanda's parents, aware of her fears, had tried to reassure her, but Amanda had continued to imagine that the very worst would happen— that Stevi would never be her sister.

"This is the room," said Amanda's dad as he opened a large wooden door. Amanda smoothed her white dress with the purple ribbon at the waist. She looked at her family. If the judge saw them like this, nothing would go wrong. After all, they were the neatest, cleanest, most dressed up they'd been in a long time. Like Daddy, Joey and Nicky wore ties. Amanda's mom had on her soft pink dress and the high heels Amanda loved to borrow. Baby Stevi looked extra special. She was wearing her pink dress and tights. Her usually fuzzy, sticking-out hair was tucked into a white bonnet trimmed with lace and ribbons. Stevi's cheeks were scrubbed and, for once, she wasn't drooling.

"This is the same courtroom we were in when we adopted you, Amanda," said her mother as she followed Amanda into the room. "As I recall, we wait in here until the judge calls us into his chamber or office."

"Was I here, too?" asked Nicky, his eyes wide with interest.

"No, Nicky," said Mom. "We adopted you in the same building, but I think it was a different room. If we have time, we can go look for it."

Amanda didn't remember anything about her own adoption or Nicky's. Joey had been adopted in Mexico and only Mom and Dad had been there.

Amanda's mom waved at a pretty, blond woman who looked familiar to Amanda. It was Liz, the social worker. Amanda smiled and waved, too. Liz was there to help the family adopt Stevi. She would be asked by the judge to answer some questions.

As the family and Liz took seats on a bench that looked like a church pew, Amanda noticed that everyone was acting quiet and respectful as they would in church, even Nicky.

She looked around. The room was full of adults with little kids. They were all colors and sizes. Some of the kids looked older than Amanda. She tapped her dad's shoulder and whispered, "Dad, are all these kids going to be adopted today?"

"Maybe some are waiting to adopt younger brothers or sisters," he answered. "But some are kids, older than you, who are being adopted."

Amanda look carefully at the people around her. From behind, she heard a mother's voice whisper, "Sit up straight." She turned to look. A very pretty woman was fixing an older boy's tie. He looked like he didn't want to be in court.

Amanda turned around. She noticed that the family in front of her was black. A cute little girl sat between her mother and father. Her hair was braided with bright ribbons and barrettes at the tops and bottoms of the braids.

Mom and Dad talked quietly with Liz. Baby Stevi was curled in her mother's arms. She was wide awake and looking at all the new sights. Joey, who was sitting between Amanda and Nicky, sucked quietly on his bottle and stared around the big room. Nicky, like Amanda, was busy taking in the grand surroundings of a real courtroom.

Tall, thin windows lined one wall. Wood paneling covered the other walls. A desk stood high above everything in the room. A railing separated the benches from the desk and two tables. Amanda noticed a door on the opposite wall. A sign read "Judge Even." She swung her legs and began to watch the waiting people. Nicky pulled on his tie, then curled it up and pulled it out again. Amanda hoped the wait wouldn't be too long. She didn't think the babies could be quiet all afternoon.

A man came out of the judge's door. "Munson," he called. "Mr. and Mrs. Munson, and Arthur." Two short parents and a boy who looked about Amanda's age followed the blue-suited man through the door. It closed again.

Amanda continued to watch the people. It was taking longer than she wanted it to. The babies wouldn't last. What if they started to act fussy, Amanda wondered. Would the judge say no to the adoption if Joey and Stevi started acting tired and crabby? She crossed her legs. She uncrossed them. Amanda was getting tired of waiting.

Baby Stevi began to fuss. Amanda's mom passed her over to Dad, then rummaged through the diaper bag. An empty bottle hung in Joey's mouth as he walked back and forth on the long, wooden bench.

Nicky put the end of his tie in his mouth, then blew it out. Amanda swung her legs again. She watched and waited.

Every once in a while the man in the blue suit poked his head out of the judge's door and called another name. Families went in the door, and when they came out they looked the same— just happier.

This wait is getting too long, thought Amanda. I'm getting bored. So was Joey. He was getting louder and louder. He jumped up and down on the wooden bench. Mom and Dad tried to quiet him. Liz tried to play with him. Finally they all ignored him. Joey started to sing. He threw his bottle high in the air and hit his father on the head as everyone in the courtroom chuckled. Amanda scrunched down on the bench and covered her eyes with her hands. "Oh brother," she muttered.

Now Joey was chattering like a monkey and running back and forth on the ground while his dad tried to catch him. Stevi fussed for a bottle but Amanda's mother hadn't found one in the diaper bag. Nicky continued to suck his tie and giggle at Joey.

Amanda sure hoped the judge didn't come out and see them now. He'd never allow the adoption. She wondered what the judge would look like. She thought he would be the tallest man she had ever seen. He would wear a big, long black robe with sleeves that covered his hands. Amanda hoped he wasn't mean, that he'd let them keep Stevi.

"Angel," called the man. Amanda's family stood and followed him into the judge's chamber.

The room was smaller than the courtroom. A long table surrounded by chairs seemed to fill it. The judge, who was sitting at the head of the table, was just like any normal person. He wore a brown suit and glasses and smiled at the children.

Everyone was quiet. Mom and Dad sat in the chairs and were sworn in. This was a promise-to-tell-the-truth swear, not the bad-word kind. Liz, the social worker, read from a pad of paper about the family. She said Stevi would be raised in a loving home with caring brothers and a caring sister. Amanda liked that part. Then the judge asked Amanda's parents questions like, "How old are you?" and, "What are your full, legal names?" At last he asked Amanda's parents if they wanted to raise Stephanie Jean as their own child for the rest of their lives. Although he used many complicated legal words, Amanda was sure that was what he meant. Her parents quickly replied, "Yes."

"Let the record show the adoption is granted," said the judge. Amanda thought the next part was the neatest. The judge looked right at her and said, "You children were so good, your parents should take you out for ice cream."

Amanda was surprised and pleased that her parents took the family and Liz to a dress-up kind of restaurant and they had grilled cheese sandwiches with fancy, curled up carrot decorations. They ate and finished up with ice cream— except for Stevi, who had fallen asleep in her mother's arms.

After ice cream and a warm good-by to Liz, the family relaxed at home.

Amanda and her mom sat in the wicker rocking chair on the porch and watched Stevi roll on the blanket, trying to catch a sunbeam.

"Does this mean Stevi's ours now?" asked Amanda.

Amanda's mom knew exactly what she meant. "Yes, Honey. Stevi is your sister and she's our beautiful daughter for ever and ever."

"For sure she's my real sister?"

"For sure."

"No one can ever change their mind?" asked Amanda.

"No one. Ever."

Amanda hopped from the chair and knelt on the floor and hugged her fuzzy-haired, round, brown baby. "You're finally my sister," whispered Amanda. She didn't tell Stevi she was sorry that once she had wanted only a brother. She didn't tell Stevi that she was sorry for ignoring her. And Amanda didn't tell baby Stevi that she loved her as much as anyone could love a sister. She thought it though.

Baby Stevi reached out and grabbed Amanda's nose as Amanda reached to tickle her bare toes. Dad and the boys could be heard as they wrestled in the grass. Sun streamed onto the porch. Amanda was a very happy big sister.

I wonder, she thought. I just wonder if Mom and Dad are ready for another baby.

Amanda knew she was.

ABOUT THE AUTHOR

Ann Angel is a mother, writer and journalism instructor who has written extensively about adoption related issues. Her articles have included researched and interview-based subjects such as children's searches for their birthparents, bi-racial and inter-country adoption and, now, REAL FOR SURE SISTER, a personal perspective of family love and adoption.

She has also written and researched numerous business and feature articles for local magazines, newspapers and academic publications. But the subject of family and parenting is a constant focus for Ann, who draws upon personal experience as a starting point in writing about sibling rivalry, parenting psychology and the psychology of raising children.

Ann received her undergraduate degree from Mount Mary College in Milwaukee, Wisconsin where she is presently teaching journalism and advising the student newspaper. She received an MA in Journalism from Marquette University in Milwaukee. Ann also teaches non-fiction writing at The Great Lakes Writers Workshop at Alverno College in Milwaukee and is working on another juvenile novel.

Ann, her husband, Jeff, and their four children live in Wauwatosa, Wisconsin. Although the children, who were adopted at birth from the United States and Mexico, served as models for REAL FOR SURE SISTER, the book is fiction.

ILLUSTRATOR

Joanne Bowring is the mother of a Korean born daughter, Mary Won Hee, 3, followed by Timothy, 1, her birth son. Joanne is a commercial artist with a Milwaukee, Wisconsin, ad agency. In her spare time, she is a free lance illustrator specializing in whimsical children's drawings. Joanne has handled all artists' media including photography, graphics materials and her specialty, watercolors. She attended Mount Mary College and holds a BA in commercial art from the University of Wisconsin - Stevens Point.

Joanne, her husband, Doug, and their children live in Wauwatosa, Wisconsin.

LET US INTRODUCE OURSELVES...

Perspectives Press is a narrowly focused publishing company. The materials we produce or distribute all speak to issues related to infertility or to adoption. Our purpose is to promote understanding of these issues and to educate and sensitize those personally experiencing these life situations, professionals who work in infertility and adoption, and the public at large. Perspectives Press titles are never duplicative. We seek out and publish materials that are currently unavailable through traditional sources. Our titles include . . .

Perspectives on a Grafted Tree

An Adoptor's Advocate

Understanding: A Guide to Impaired Fertility for Family and Friends

Our Baby: A Birth and Adoption Story

Our Child: Preparation for Parenting in Adoption

The Special Event Planbook

The Mulberry Bird

The Miracle Seekers: An Anthology of Infertility

Our authors have special credentials: they are people whose personal and professional lives provide an interwoven pattern for what they write. If **you** are writing about infertility or adoption, we invite you to contact us with a query letter and stamped, self addressed envelope so that we can send you our writers guidelines and help you determine whether your materials might fit into our publishing scheme.

Perspectives Press
905 West Wildwood Avenue
Fort Wayne, IN 46807